Merry Christmas Kevin
12-25-86

Grandpa
and
Grandma
Hackney

MOON
OF THE BIG-DOG

MOON
OF THE BIG-DOG

by JAY LEECH and ZANE SPENCER

Illustrated by MAMORU FUNAI

Thomas Y. Crowell   New York

Acknowledgment

This story is based, in part, on a legend as re-counted by Mari Sandoz in *Love Song to the Plains*, copyright © 1961 by Mari Sandoz, published by Harper and Row.

Text copyright © 1980 by Jay Leech and Zane Spencer
Illustrations copyright © 1980 by Mamoru Funai
All rights reserved. Printed in the United States of America.
No part of this book may be used or reproduced in any manner
whatsoever without written permission except in the case of
brief quotations embodied in critical articles and reviews.
For information address Thomas Y. Crowell, 10 East 53rd Street,
New York, N.Y. 10022. Published simultaneously in Canada by
Fitzhenry & Whiteside Limited, Toronto.
Designed by Amelia Lau

Library of Congress Cataloging in Publication Data

Leech, Jay, 1931–
Moon of the big-dog.
SUMMARY: A retelling of the legend which describes
how the Brulé Indians got their name.
1. Brulé Indians—Legends. 2. Indians of North
America—Great Plains—Legends. [1. Brulé Indians—
Legends. 2. Indians of North America—Great Plains—
Legends] I. Spencer, Zane, 1935– joint author.
II. Funai, Mamoru. III. Title.
E99.B8L43   398.2′09′78   79-7893
ISBN 0-690-04001-6   ISBN 0-690-04002-4 lib. bdg.

10 9 8 7 6 5 4 3 2 1
First Edition

Dedicated to our children
in the order of their appearance:
Stephanie, Laurie, Mark,
Michael, Matthew, and Leeann.

Contents

There are many legends about how the Brule Sioux got their name. This story is based on one of them.

The events told here happened back when the Teton Sioux still lived in the Minnesota region. Each year a few young braves who had just earned their first feathers of manhood were chosen to make the six-hundred-mile journey to the trading grounds near the North Platte River in western Nebraska. The braves were entrusted with the crafts made by the women of the village. At the fair, they were to barter wisely for the wares of distant tribes.

The trading grounds were a place of general truce where friends and enemies came together in peace. For twenty-eight days—the time of one full moon to the next—they traded, feasted, and danced. Old men smoked the pipe of friendship and told and retold stories of brave deeds. Young men competed in foot races and wrestling matches, and showed off their skills with bows and arrows. Men and women alike wagered on the contests.

This is the story of three young braves who were chosen to make the journey one year. It was a journey that was to change the way of life for the Teton Sioux. We call it here the "moon of the big-dog."

The Parting

Black Raven rubbed the sleep from his eyes. It was still dark in the tepee. He could hear the soft snoring of his father, Bold Eagle. His mother was asleep, too. So were his three young brothers.

Get up, Black Raven wanted to shout. This is the day that Strong Bow and Young Turtle and I leave for the trading fair.

He wondered if Strong Bow and Young Turtle were feeling the same excitement. They must be, he decided. This would be their first journey away from the tribe, too. Black Raven felt a surge of pride. He and his friends were no longer small boys. This was an important journey. This was the year they would do the trading for their tribe.

Then Black Raven remembered what he had overheard yesterday. Some of the women had been talking together as they scraped buffalo hides. . . .

"Every summer it is the same," Bird Woman said, shaking her head. "We must trust our finest handwork to young men who are hardly more than boys."

"Yes," Straight Willow said. "I would rather have the older men trade for me. Men who know what they are doing."

"Did you see Black Raven miss that deer the other morning?" Old Grandmother said. "It was standing right at the edge of the village. Black Raven waved everybody aside like a great hunter claiming his prize." She clicked her tongue as she scraped at the hide in front of her. "And then he missed. That arrow may still be flying, for all I know. I do know it didn't hit the deer. . . ."

The women had laughed. Black Raven could still hear them. Why do they only remember the mistake I made? he wondered. Why don't they remember all the deer I hit, instead of the one I missed?

Well, it didn't matter now. He would show them. He would show everyone. He would bring back finer goods from the trading fair than any of the other braves who had gone before.

Black Raven opened the flap of the tepee and slipped outside. It was still dark. The moon hung low in the sky. It was a full moon, and that was always a good sign. Everything would go well on the journey. He stretched and looked around the village. It was quiet. Even the dogs were still asleep.

Wake up, Black Raven wanted to yell. It is time for the journey to begin. But no, he could not do that. Only children squeal and jump up and down.

Instead, he ran for the stream and jumped into the water. It was fresh and cold and it felt good against his bare skin. He had been in the stream for only a few minutes when Strong Bow leaped over the bushes and joined him.

"Where is Young Turtle?" Black Raven asked.

"I called to him as I passed his tepee," said Strong Bow. "But he didn't answer. You know him. A grizzly bear could pull the world down around him and he wouldn't wake up."

When Black Raven returned from his morning swim, his mother was busy cooking breakfast. She added dried meat and ground corn to the water in the cooking pouch. Then she started it boiling by adding hot stones.

Next she packed the goods she would send to the fair. She folded ermine pelts and elaborate shirts and moccasins decorated with her fine quillwork. She tied them into bundles. Then she tied the bundles to the travois poles.

Black Raven knew it was not proper to help his mother do her work. But he was too eager to just wait and watch. He rechecked the pack he would carry.

He tucked in the extra moccasins his mother had made. He sharpened his knife again and tested his bow. Then he looked to the east. The sun had never taken so long to rise.

When at last it did and it was time to leave, Black Raven, Strong Bow, and Young Turtle stood in the center of the village. One by one the women of the tribe led their rough-haired pack dogs to them and handed over the lead thongs.

"These are my finest goods. I worked hard to make them," Bird Woman said, and she patted the bundle on the travois behind her dog. "You trade well and bring me a fine woven blanket of many colors from the hot country people."

"And the bright copper metal that can glow like embers," said another woman.

"I want the black glass stone from the far west land," Straight Willow said.

Old Grandmother pushed her way forward. "Bring three things." She raised her bony hand and

checked off a finger for each as she spoke. "The nut of the piñon, the green and blue feathers, and the herbs for healing." She wagged her fingers at them. "Only three things. You remember, now!"

Black Raven nodded. "We will remember, Old Grandmother. Three things."

Her three bony fingers still extended, she waved the young men on their way. "Remember, now," she called after them.

"The nut of the piñon," Strong Bow called.

"Green and blue feathers," Black Raven called.

"And don't forget my herbs for healing," Old Grandmother called to them again.

"We will remember," Young Turtle called back.

Bold Eagle walked with the young braves as far as the stream. "Travel with the eyes of the hawk," he said. "At the trading fair all tribes come together in peace. But on the way there is much danger. There are some who would take your scalps and steal the trade goods."

Black Raven wanted to get going. His father had already told him all these things over and over. Still, he knew he must be polite, so he tried to pay attention.

"When you reach the great buffalo plain there will be no landmark to guide you," he went on. "The earth will seem the same day after day. Use the sun as your guide. Shoot an arrow ahead of you to keep your direction straight. Those who have gone before you have left stone and buffalo-skull markers. Watch for them." At last he said good-bye. "May Wankan Tanka and all the other good spirits go with you," he called after them.

Black Raven led the way. Young Turtle and Strong Bow followed. They urged the dogs across the stream and made their way through the trees.

"We are on our way at last," Black Raven shouted. "Ooweee!"

"Ooweee!" Strong Bow and Young Turtle joined in.

The dogs yapped and barked. They were excited, too.

"This is going to be the best journey ever," Black Raven shouted, and his voice sang through the woods.

The Journey

For many days they traveled through shaded woodland paths. They knew these trails well. They had traveled them many times on hunting parties. Each night they took turns guarding their camp.

"Stay awake and stay alert," they cautioned each other. "We can't let anyone steal the trade goods."

". . . Or take our scalps," Young Turtle always added.

As they traveled, the trees of the forest grew thinner. At last one day they came to the place where there were no trees at all. They stood at the edge of the wide buffalo land.

Black Raven shielded his eyes to look across the

13

plains. He could see no landmarks. There was not a single tree by which he could set a course. He did not see the rock piles or buffalo skulls his father had said to look for. There was only a great sea of dull green-gray grass waving in the wind.

For a long moment he studied the sun in the sky. Then he pulled an arrow from his quiver. He tied three feathers to the notched end of the shaft. Then he strung his bow and set an arrow. He aimed high above the horizon and sent the arrow cutting through the air. The point landed in the ground and the feathers fluttered in the soft wind. The braves started toward them. When they reached the arrow, Black Raven pulled it from the ground. He looked at the sun and shot the arrow toward the southwest again.

"Do you think we will ever get there?" Young Turtle asked. "Maybe we are lost."

"We are not lost," Black Raven said.

"Well, maybe we are not lost," Strong Bow said, "but we are traveling so slowly that there won't be anything left to trade for when we get there. Or maybe the fair will even be over."

In the days that followed, Black Raven urged the weary dogs to move faster. They hunted as they traveled. When they were lucky, there was plump prairie chicken or even an occasional young buck for their night meal.

It was midsummer now. The flat land had changed to great hills. A full moon and half of another had passed since they had started their journey. Now sometimes they could see other travelers in the distance. They were all moving in the same direction, toward the great trading fair.

Then, late one day, they saw it. Stretched out before them, not a half day's journey from where they stood, was the huge camp of the trading grounds. It sprawled out along the banks of a winding creek as far as their eyes could see. The smoke of many cooking fires hung in the air.

"There it is!" Black Raven cried.

Strong Bow cheered and Young Turtle ran in cir-
cles, leaping like a grasshopper.

With a big sigh, Strong Bow fell in a heap in the
long grass. Black Raven sat down beside him. He
spoke earnestly. "We will get everything our people
asked for—the finest goods ever. We will show them
they sent men, not boys, to do their trading for them."

Young Turtle wagged his finger and made his
voice waver. "And don't forget my herbs for healing.
Three things. Remember."

They all laughed.

Suddenly one of the dogs started barking wildly.
The rest of the pack quickly joined in. Their teeth
were bared. Their hackles were raised. A strange
creature had leaped out of a dry wash in the distance. It was racing toward them. They were being
attacked by a huge monster.

It was coming so fast they knew it would be useless
to run. Quickly they strung their bows, set their arrows, and made a line of defense.

The beast thundered toward them. It shook the ground beneath their feet. Their hearts beat with fear as the unknown danger pounded nearer and nearer. They aimed their bows, tensed their muscles, and waited for the monster to come within range of their arrows.

The Big-Dog

"Hold steady. Wait until it is closer!" Black Raven commanded. "We will have only one shot."

Strong Bow and Young Turtle stood ready. They both nodded, waiting. Then they saw the monster—half giant dog and half man—raise its hand as it charged toward them.

"Not yet," Black Raven said.

The dog-monster slowed its pace. It was still out of range.

"Come on!" Strong Bow taunted courageously. "We are ready!"

At the sound of Strong Bow's voice, the dog-monster stopped.

Black Raven relaxed his bow slowly. "Don't shoot. The big dog-monster means us no harm. See, its hand is raised in the sign of peace. We must go out and see."

"Not me." Young Turtle shook his head. "That could be an evil spirit tricking us."

"I don't think it is a trick. I believe it is a man . . . on the biggest dog I have ever seen." Black Raven's eyes were wide with amazement.

Strong Bow took a step closer and shielded his eyes for a better look. "You may be right," he said.

"It's a trick," Young Turtle cautioned, but he, too, had begun to relax his bow.

Slowly Black Raven started forward. The other two followed.

"See, it is not a monster," Black Raven said, and he raised his hand in the sign of friendship. "It is an Apache brave. But what is he riding?"

The three youths stared. The man on the back of the strange animal spoke. "Horse," he said, pointing to the beast.

"Horse?" Black Raven repeated the strange word. "Horse," he said again, and he dared to touch the giant creature. "See how gentle it is," he said as he stroked the huge black animal.

Young Turtle put out his hand to touch it, too. "It is so soft," he whispered.

"It is the most beautiful animal I have ever seen," Black Raven said. "I wish my father, Bold Eagle, could see it."

Suddenly the Apache dug his heels into the horse's sides. The animal wheeled and reared.

The Apache laughed. "I will race you to the camp!" Then the horse with its rider galloped away, its hooves pounding hard against the earth.

Black Raven watched until the beautiful creature disappeared again into the dry wash. He was filled with a feeling he could not explain. Not even to himself.

It was nearly dark when the three Sioux braves reached the trading grounds. Quickly they set up their camp.

"Let's go to the dancing," Young Turtle said.

"You and Strong Bow go ahead. I will join you later." Black Raven waved them on their way. Then he started toward the Apache camp. He had to see the horse again.

In the pale moonlight he saw the dark shapes of many horses. They were tied at the edge of the Apache camp. Quietly he slipped along the picket line until he found the black one. He touched its soft muzzle. He ran his hand over the powerful muscles of its body. He spoke softly to the great beast. The horse nickered in gentle reply.

"You are the most beautiful animal," Black Raven whispered, and he laid his head gently against the horse's neck. He stayed there until the wild dancing drums grew quiet and the storytelling fires turned to ashes. He stayed there until the gray light of dawn crept into the eastern sky. Then he returned to his camp.

In the early morning hours, a vision came to Black Raven. A great bird, a black raven, appeared to him. It was from such a black raven that he had taken his manhood name many moons ago. It flew above the black horse, circling until it came to rest on the horse's back. Suddenly another horse appeared beside the first one. And another. And another. Then the raven flew across the plains, back toward the Teton Sioux village. And the horses followed.

Then Black Raven saw himself. The raven was with him once more. He tried to speak to it. But the raven didn't answer. It gave one mighty flap of its wings and, sleek as an arrow, flew straight into the rising sun.

The Vision

The vision ended, but the restless sleep went on.

When Strong Bow woke up he said, "We looked for you at the dancing last night. Where were you?"

"I went to see the horses," Black Raven answered, as he shook himself awake. The vision was still close upon him. He covered his face with his hands and tried to recall it.

"What's the matter?" Young Turtle asked. "Are you sick?"

"No." Black Raven shook his head. "I had a vision from Wankan Tanka, the Great Spirit, and I'm trying to figure out what it means."

"A vision?" Interest sparked in Strong Bow's eyes. "I'm good at understanding visions. Tell us about it."

Strong Bow and Young Turtle came close to hear their friend. When he had finished talking, they looked at him with puzzled expressions.

Young Turtle frowned. "Do you know what it means, Strong Bow?"

Strong Bow shook his head. "No. I don't know. What do *you* think it means, Black Raven?"

Black Raven was silent for a long moment. Then he stamped his foot on the ground in sudden excitement. "The horses! We are going to get the horses!"

"What?" cried Strong Bow and Young Turtle together.

"The vision!" said Black Raven urgently. "I think it means we are supposed to trade for horses."

"We can't do that!" Young Turtle exclaimed. "If we go back home with horses instead of the things we were sent to get, the women will boil us for supper."

"And besides," added Strong Bow, "we don't have enough goods for even one horse. I heard at the dancing that the Apaches are asking much for the big animals. How could we do it?"

"I don't know," Black Raven said. "But the Great Spirit gave me a vision. Somehow we will find a way to get the horses. I am sure of it."

"Well, *I* am not sure," Young Turtle protested. "And I don't understand the whole thing. The horses are beautiful, but why do we need them? Why would the Great Spirit want us to have them?"

"Two horses would be the beginning of a great herd. The horses are strong. They can pull heavier loads than dogs." Black Raven's voice rose, and he waved his arms as he spoke. "With horses we could hunt the buffalo more easily, and in battle we could move with the speed of the wind."

"Yes!" Strong Bow cried, catching Black Raven's enthusiasm.

But Young Turtle put his hands to his head. "The

women will never understand," he moaned, "and neither will my father."

"They will," Black Raven assured him. "I know they will once they see what the horses can do."

"But we still don't have enough trade goods," Strong Bow reminded him.

"Then we will get more," said Black Raven. "We can start with the contests. There are many for us to enter, and the prizes are valuable. All we have to do is win."

The Apache

The days of the trading fair became a race against time. Strong Bow was right—the Apaches were asking much for their horses. But the winning of the prizes had become an adventure. Even Young Turtle was caught up in it. The young braves won many things to add to the trade goods they had brought from home, but it seemed as if they would never have enough.

Then one morning Black Raven said to his friends, "The fair is almost over. We will make a bargain today. We know the two horses we want."

They gathered their trade goods and marched to

the Apache camp. "The chestnut and the black," Black Raven announced, and he pointed to the two horses they had chosen.

The Apache trader looked at the three young braves and laughed. "You do not have enough goods for two such fine horses."

"Let us show you what we have," Black Raven said confidently.

First he offered his mother's fine quillwork. The Apache fingered it and then shook his head. "Not enough. That one"—he pointed to the chestnut mare —"is in foal. She will have a colt in the spring."

Slowly Black Raven added the rest of the trade goods, one piece at a time.

The Apache looked and admired, but always he shook his head and said, "Not enough."

When everything—the white ermine pelts, the precious red pipestone, the copper necklaces, all the prizes won in the games, and even the valuable pack dogs—had been offered, and the Apache had said,

"Not enough," each time, Young Turtle leaned over and whispered to Black Raven, "There is nothing more. We will have to give up."

"We have nothing left to trade," Strong Bow added. "What else can we do?"

For a long moment Black Raven didn't answer. He stood looking toward the morning sun, remembering his vision. They had tried so hard. They couldn't go home now without the horses. What could they do?

Slowly a thought formed. He turned and grinned at his two friends. "I have an idea," he said, pulling Strong Bow and Young Turtle into a huddle. He began to whisper. When he finished, he stepped back. "It will work," he said. "I know it will if we do it right."

"Do you think we can?" Strong Bow said.

"Think about it." Black Raven was excited.

"It would be a great risk," Young Turtle said.

"But it just might work," Strong Bow mused. "Let's try it."

33

The Wager

"Stop!" Black Raven called to the Apache, who had started to walk away. He was laughing and joking with the group of braves around him.

At the sound of Black Raven's voice he turned. "Whatever it is," he said, still laughing, "it is not enough."

Black Raven caught up to him. "No . . . yes. Listen. I will make a wager with you," he said.

"Wager?" A gleam of interest flashed across the Apache's face.

"I'll wager that my friend, Strong Bow, can shoot the arrow truer than anyone in your tribe."

The Apache laughed louder and slapped his knee. "I am the best bowman in my tribe. So what will you lose to me?"

"We will wager all of our trade goods for the two horses."

"I told you that you don't have enough goods."

Black Raven spoke boldly. "If the Apache is afraid of the Sioux arrow, I will make the wager even better. If you win, you will have everything. If we win, you can still have all the trade goods, but we will get the horses."

The wager had now become a challenge. The Apache could not refuse, and Black Raven knew it.

"The young Sioux speaks with the voice of a man," the Apache said loudly. "But can his friend shoot an arrow like one?"

"That you will know tomorrow when the sun rises," Black Raven said. "Each archer will shoot three arrows at a target. The arrow that hits closest to the center will win."

The Apache smiled broadly and nodded in agreement.

Now it was Black Raven who smiled. The Apache had accepted the challenge. The horses were as good as theirs, for Strong Bow was surely the best bowman at the fair. He had won every contest he had entered.

Word of the wager spread quickly around the camp. Early the next morning a crowd had already gathered when the three young Sioux arrived at the shooting range.

"It looks like everyone at the fair is here," Young Turtle said. "Already they are making bets with one another."

Black Raven nodded. "Here comes the Apache."

"What if I miss?" Strong Bow rubbed his hands together nervously.

"You never miss," Black Raven assured his friend.

"You are a good marksman too, but you missed that deer at the edge of our camp. Do you remember?"

"How could I forget?" Black Raven smiled at the memory, even though it was still a little painful to him. "You are a better bowman than I am. You will not miss."

The Apache walked closer.

"Are you ready?" Black Raven asked.

"I am ready," the Apache said. "But I have another condition to the wager."

"We agreed to the terms yesterday," Black Raven protested.

"My horses are very valuable. If you wish to go on with the contest, you will meet my condition."

"What is the new condition?"

"It must be you who shoots the arrows, not your friend."

"Me?" Black Raven stepped back. "Why me?"

"It is you who speaks loudest about owning the

horses for your tribe. You should have the honor of winning them."

Black Raven tried to think of a way around this new condition. The Apache had been clever with his words. Black Raven could hardly refuse the challenge. If he did, he would appear to be a coward and bring shame upon himself and his tribe.

"No," Young Turtle whispered. "You can't accept."

"We could lose everything," Strong Bow cautioned.

Thoughts of the missed deer flashed across Black Raven's mind. But the thought of the horses was stronger. Once more he looked toward the morning sun and remembered his vision. The vision had told him to trade for the horses. Was there something else? In his mind he saw again the black raven on its sleek flight into the sun. And then he knew.

"I agree," he said to the Apache. "But I also have a condition."

"And what is that?" The Apache smiled broadly.

"The target. It must be placed in the direction of the morning sun."

"We will not be able to see," the Apache said. "The sun will blind our eyes."

"That is my condition," Black Raven said flatly.

The Apache shrugged. "That is foolish," he said, "but I agree."

The arrangements for the contest were made. A Cheyenne, an Ojibwa, and a Zuni were chosen to judge. They scratched a line on the dusty ground. "The arrows will be shot from here," they said.

"It is not too late. You can still back out of the contest," Young Turtle said.

"I know you are thinking about the deer I missed at the village," Black Raven said. "But remember my vision. The raven was an arrow, and it was flying straight into the sun."

"But you are not shooting at the sun. You are shooting at a buffalo hide with a circle painted on it."

"The spirits will not fail us," Black Raven said. "If it is meant for us to win the horses, we will. I know it."

"The sun is too bright. It will blind your eyes," Strong Bow added. "How can you hit a target you cannot see?"

"The Apache can't see it either," said Black Raven. He slipped his quiver from his back. Carefully he chose the three black-feathered arrows he would use.

Then the Zuni judge stepped forward. "It is decided. The Apache will shoot first," he said.

Black Raven, Young Turtle, and Strong Bow waited silently as the Apache stepped to the line. A hush fell over the crowd. The Apache took his time. He squinted against the glare of the sun. Then he drew his bow and shot. The arrow cut through the air and thudded into the target.

The men shouted. The women and girls showed their approval with high-pitched calls. Smoothly the Apache released his second and third arrows.

They, too, hit the target.

Now it was Black Raven's turn. He stepped to the line and shaded his eyes, trying to see the position of the Apache's arrows in the target. He had heard all three hit, but he could not see how close they were to the center. Slowly he raised his bow. He aimed into the glare and shot.

He waited for the thud of the arrow against the target. Instead he heard the moans of the crowd. His arrow had missed completely.

Black Raven could not look at his friends, but he could feel their eyes burning into his back. He raised the second black-feathered arrow and let the bow-string snap.

The crowd moaned again, and Black Raven's heart sank. The second arrow had also missed. Behind him Black Raven could hear the Apache's jeers. ''The young Sioux cannot even hit the target, much less the center.''

Black Raven's hands trembled as he fitted the last

arrow to his bow. His last chance. Had he been wrong about his vision? Was getting the horses only a wild dream? Was he a foolish young brave, as the women at home had said?

The sun had risen higher now, above the target. He raised his bow and said a silent prayer to Wankan Tanka, the Great Spirit. He pulled the bowstring back . . . back . . . and aimed directly into the blazing sun. Then his fingers released the string. Like the black-feathered bird in his vision, the arrow soared sleekly toward the sun.

Thud.

Amid the cries of the excited crowd, the Cheyenne, Ojibwa, and Zuni judges hurried to the target. Black Raven held his breath.

A murmur of impatience rippled through the crowd. "Who is the winner?" a man called.

Then with one quick motion the Cheyenne pulled out an arrow and held it high above his head. "It is the black feather," he shouted. "The Sioux wins."

The crowd roared. Young Turtle and Strong Bow threw their arms around Black Raven and lifted him into the air.

"We won!" they shouted. "The horses are ours!"

The Homecoming

The trading fair was over. The three young Sioux braves gathered their few belongings for the trip home.

"Our bows, our knives, and a few arrows. That is not much," Young Turtle moaned. "How can I face my father?"

"But we have the horses," Strong Bow said. "The spirits were on our side. How can your father argue with that?"

"I don't know." Young Turtle shrugged. "But I still say we will be lucky if the women do not put us in the cooking pouch and stew us up for supper."

Black Raven laughed. "They will soon see. This has been the greatest trading fair ever!" He fixed his pack of belongings on the black stallion and swung himself onto the animal's back. "Now, let's go home. Ooweee!"

They started on their way. Black Raven and Strong Bow rode double on the stallion. Young Turtle rode the chestnut mare. From the top of the rise where they had first seen the big dog-monster, they looked back toward the trading camp. The people were moving away toward their homes. Large and small parties traveled to the east and west, the north and south.

All that day they moved steadily across the prairie. It was hard for them to believe that they were moving so fast. By nightfall they had covered more ground than in three days of walking.

"Oh," moaned Young Turtle when they finally stopped to camp by a small stream. "If I had known how sore riding these big-dogs would make my body, I never would have agreed to the trade."

"And the calluses you must grow." Strong Bow winced and rubbed his backside.

Black Raven groaned. "And the sunburn! My thighs are on fire."

"Ours, too!" the other two agreed. They were already lowering their burned and aching limbs into the cool water of the stream.

The sun had traveled across the sky many times on the way to the trading fair. But now, riding horseback, they made the journey home in only a small part of that time. Soon they signaled their approach to the village. The mirror in Black Raven's hand caught the rays of the sun. "We are home," the light flashed. "We have returned."

The three young Sioux rode into sight of the camp and stopped short. The bows of their people were raised against them. They were ready to attack.

"Why do they form a line of defense?" Young Turtle asked.

"They don't believe that it is us," Black Raven said. "We are home too soon."

"Signal again," Strong Bow advised. "More than likely they are afraid of the big-dogs."

"Yes, that is it." Black Raven brought out the mirror and flashed the message again. "Do not be afraid," he added. He had grown so used to the horses that he had forgotten that terrible day on the hill when they, too, had formed a line of defense, sure that a monster was attacking them.

The three rode slowly into the village calling and shouting, "It is us. See, we are Black Raven, Strong Bow, and Young Turtle. We have come home."

At last the braves relaxed their bows, but none would venture forward. The women and children stayed hidden in their tepees. Even the dogs cowered near their owners. They yapped and barked, but took only a few timid steps toward the strange animals stalking into their domain.

"Horses," Black Raven called to the people.

"Come and see what we have brought from the fair."

"They are beautiful animals. They will not hurt you," Strong Bow pleaded.

"They are gentle . . . and most helpful." Young Turtle's voice quivered. He searched the frightened crowd for sight of his father.

Slowly the villagers came forward. First one, then another. Soon they filled the village center, standing a cautious distance from the two big animals.

Bird Woman pushed her way to the front. "But where is my blanket?" she asked.

"And the black stone? I see no bundles . . . no travois," Straight Willow called from somewhere near the back of the crowd.

"We did not bring these things, but we have made a better bargain. We traded everything for the beautiful creatures we ride. We have brought horses," Black Raven announced.

Strong Bow and Young Turtle nodded their heads and added, "A really fine bargain."

"Everything! All of our goods! Everything gone for two beasts! What do we want with two beasts?" The stunned remarks rippled through the village.

"We have been cheated!"

"A poor bargain."

"This is what we get for sending foolish boys to do the jobs of men," Bird Woman shrieked.

"My herbs for healing . . ." Old Grandmother wailed. She raised a single bony finger and waved it feebly at them.

Some of the men stood to one side and glared at the returning braves. "Burnt thighs!" one of them shouted in disgust.

Black Raven looked down at his legs. It was true. The painful red sunburn had turned to a deep tan, making his thighs much darker than the rest of his skin.

"I told you the people would be angry with us," Young Turtle whispered.

"Talk to them," Strong Bow said. "Tell them about

your vision. Tell them what the big-dogs can do. Convince them as you convinced Young Turtle and me. Make them understand."

Black Raven raised his head and swallowed hard. "They will understand," he said, and he slid to the ground. "Come on. We will tell them together."

And slowly the three braves led the horses into the waiting crowd.

The people of the Teton Sioux village were **not** totally convinced that day. But gradually, as the horses made their lives easier, they did agree. The three young braves had made a wise decision.

The horses multiplied into a great herd and their fame spread. The French traders called their owners Brules, Burnt Thigh Men (from **brulées cuisses**, meaning "burnt thighs"). The creek near which the trading grounds were located became known as the River of the Horses, or Horse Creek. Hundreds of years later it was part of the last hunting grounds of the Brule Sioux, great horsemen of the plains.

Also by Jay Leech and Zane Spencer
Bright Fawn and Me